Hannah's Heart
Written and Illustrated by Diane Iverson

This book is dedicated to the memory of Juan Gomez, a kindhearted man from my hometown,
and to my maternal grandparents, Virgil and Lula Mae Wall, who lived simply and with compassion.
Diane Iverson

Forward

The Great Depression was a time of extreme financial hardship for many. In America, it lasted from October 1929 through 1939. After the stock market crash of 1929, roughly 9,000 banks failed. Millions of investors lost their life savings. At its most difficult point, in 1933, the Great Depression left almost 25% of Americans out of work. Many people went hungry. Others lost their homes and everything of value.

Herbert Hoover (1874-1964) was the 31st president of the United States. He served from 1929, the year the Great Depression began, through 1933. He lost the next election to Franklin Delano Roosevelt (1882-1945), who served three full terms as President, from 1933-1945, when he died. During his first term in office, he started many social programs that helped create jobs for workers, feed families and provide other vital citizen protections. This effort was called the New Deal.

During this very hard time, families survived by being creative and resourceful. People sold things they could do without or bartered skills they had for services they needed. If one family had chickens and their neighbor had a cow, they traded eggs for milk. Many children worked at jobs they could find to help their families pay the bills.

It was a time when jobless people traveled from the hardest hit areas of the United States to other better off parts of the country in search of work, often hopping rides on freight trains.

This story is historical fiction, but the struggles of the times were very real. Prescott, Arizona, a small ranching town, suffered during the Great Depression just like the rest of the country. Most of the stores, churches and other landmarks are actual places that still exist to this day. The people in this story are typical of folks who helped each other survive the Great Depression, but with the exception of the Methodist minister, they are all entirely fictional.

Chapter One

Those were terrible hard times all across our country, and a lot of people were struggling right here in the small ranching town of Prescott, Arizona. I've never seen such sufferin' before or since. Mama used to hang her tea bag on the clothesline to dry so she could use it again, and Papa only had one cup of coffee on the weekends he was able to come home from workin' on the ranch. I don't expect us kids knew half the things Mama and Papa did to get us through those years. There was just not much work to be found and food was always a struggle for a house full of growing children.

I do remember well the Christmas of 1935. We went shoppin' at the Bashford & Burmister Company in downtown Prescott, just across from the courthouse square. It had three floors and every imaginable thing you could dream of buyin'. I was ten years old, nearly eleven, the oldest of five kids. Wesley was nine. Elizabeth was seven. Mattie turned five the month before, and Jesse was three. They were like stair-steps behind me. I was old enough to understand that Santa was havin' it just as hard as all our neighbors, but Elizabeth was dreaming of the Shirley Temple doll with the red and white dress that was lookin' back at her through the B&B Company display window. Wesley had his nose pressed against the glass, too, his eye on a Buck Rogers Space Ship. Seemed every last one of 'em was havin' grand ideas of what Santa might be bringin' the Meadows children.

"Look at the baby doll," Mattie said. "Do you think Santa would bring me that baby doll?"

"Bear," Jesse said, standing on his toes and spreading his slobber fingers flat on the cold glass, to see the display of Christmas toys. "Dat bear."

"Get your fingers off the glass, Jesse," I said. "Mama will be right back." I took Jesse's chubby wet fingers and held his hand, steppin' away from the window display.

"Hannah, how many days 'til Christmas?" Mattie asked, rubbin' her hands together to warm her fingers.

"Twenty-six days," I answered, "and stop standin' on the sides of your shoes. You'll ruin 'em, and then you won't have any." I was smart enough not to stand on the sides of my shoes, but the bottoms were near gone. I'd been lining them with cardboard like Papa did with his boots, but I was growin' so fast they weren't gonna fit much longer.

"What you think Santa's gonna bring us for Christmas, Hannah?" Wesley asked.

"I'm thinkin' Santa's first concern will be feedin' his elves and reindeer, Wes. We'll have to wait and see." He frowned back at me like I'd personally told Santa to skip our house.

We were lucky that Papa was a ranch hand, and big ranches were busy puttin' up new fencing after The Taylor Grazing Act of 1934 made public land available for lease. Papa had steady work since the ranch recently bought more Herefords to expand their stock. Still, nobody was makin' much and nobody was too sure what tomorrow might hold.

Mama came out of the store with one small package. Me bein' most grown up of the kids, I figured she'd tell me what it was soon enough, but I was sure it wasn't a doll or a rocket ship.

"We need to go to the grocery store," Mama told us, and she picked up Jesse so we could walk a bit faster.

"Button your coat, Wesley, or you'll catch your death of cold. Hannah, can you hold this package while I carry the baby?"

"Yes Ma'am." The package was light, and I tried to guess what it was as we headed toward the small grocery store on Cortez Street where Mama had a credit account with Mr. Goldstein. Almost nobody was doing credit anymore, so Mama said it was important not to abuse the kindness.

While Wesley was buttoning his coat crooked, I was thinkin' on ways I might be of some help to Santa.

Chapter Two

The next evening I was settin' the table for supper. Mama was real good with needlework, and one of her embroidery pieces hung on the wall next to the kitchen table. It was all laid out with fine French knots, graceful loops and colorful flowers. It was part of a verse from the Bible, Micah, as I recall, "...do justice, love mercy, walk humbly...." Mama loved sayin's, and there was at least one of 'em hangin' in every room. Suppose that's not much since our house was pretty small for a family of seven. The kitchen was warm and fragrant, with the wood stove cookin' buttermilk biscuits and the cast iron skillet bubblin' with milk gravy.

"Sure makes me hungry," I said to Mama as she stirred.

"It's filling," she said. Mama's hair was dark as Papa's coffee. It was parted to one side, and she pushed back the soft finger waves that fell forward as she worked over the heat of the stove. "Can you get a pint of applesauce from the cellar?" A pint was just enough to give us each a taste. Mama put up lots of fruit and vegetables from our garden, so we ate better than some of our neighbors.

"Yes, Ma'am." I headed for the back door then turned back. "Mama? Mrs. Nelson is needin' help splittin' fire wood. Suppose she would hire me to do it?"

"Hannah, that's no job for a young girl. Besides, there are plenty of men could use the work." She smiled at me. "Don't believe I've ever heard you offer to help Papa with the three cords of wood waitin' in our own shed."

That was sure enough true, so I grabbed my coat off the rack and went after the applesauce. It was gettin' near dark outside and the air was crisp, a little wind blowin'. I pulled my coat tight around me and reached for the heavy hatch door that covered the steps to the cellar. That's when I heard men talkin' in our front yard. It sounded like they were bangin' their way up the front porch steps.

"Now don't be a darn fool, James," one of 'em said. "You can't stand on it, so let us help. Best get yourself to the doctor in the mornin', and keep off it 'til you do."

"Well, now, don't be makin' such a fuss over nothin'." That was Papa, and Papa only came home from the ranch about once or twice a month, dependin' on the season. He tried to make it to church every Sunday he could, but there's lots a work to do on a big ranch.

"What in heavens' name is going on?" Mama was on the porch with them now. "James! What's happened to your leg?"

"Evening, Mrs. Meadows. Horse got spooked, I'm afraid. Leg looks to be broke. Needs checkin' come mornin'."

It didn't sound good at all. I ran down the basement steps for the applesauce so as not to miss out on anything inside. Papa had been a steady ranch hand out to one of the big ranches for years. By the time I came through the back door all breathless, the men were gone, Papa was sittin' on the couch with his foot up, and Mama was standin' in the middle of the room holdin' one of his dusty boots.

"Hannah," Mama said, "Put supper on the table for me. I'm gonna get the doctor."

She turned to Papa, "Now you stay put, James. I'll be back before you know it. I expect we'll be takin' you to Mercy Hospital to get you fixed up right." Then she was out the door. Soon enough I heard Papa's ol' 1928 Model A pickup sputterin' to life.

I settled the kids at the kitchen table and pulled the biscuits down from the warming shelf above the stove. Then I dished up the first plate, ladlin' gravy on the open biscuits, and took it to Papa.

"Think I'll wait a bit, Hannah. Thanks. Take care of the young'uns 'fore supper gets cold."

"What happened, Papa?" Wesley asked.

"Well, Wes, this here mountain lion come down off a tall granite ledge while we was ridin' the fence line, big as my horse an' twice as mean. Spooked ol' Molly somethin' awful, and she decided she could get away quicker without me weighin' her down." Papa was tellin' one of his tall tales. "So I had no choice but to wrestle that ol' lion with my bare hands 'til she gave up and run off cryin'...."

"She bite you, Papa?" Lizzy asked, all serious. She still believed Papa's stories.

"No, Lizzy. That lion was no match for me! Yer Papa's one tough ol' cowboy. Was Molly that stomped me good 'fore she took off. That's what did the damage. Darned inconsiderate horse, ol' Molly! Now y'all go on and eat."

Papa laid his head back on the sofa. His face was all pale with the pain of that leg, but he closed his eyes to wait for the doctor.

Chapter Three

It was almost time to leave for the one mile walk downtown to Washington School. Wes was out back gatherin' eggs. As I washed the breakfast dishes and Elizabeth dried, I asked Mama if she could spare some quilt scraps. She always said I was good at nice small stitches, and I thought I had a real smart way to make us some money for Christmas.

"All my quilt scraps are pretty much used up. I've been savin' up feed sacks and such for clothes," she said. "I'm afraid there's no fabric to spare, Hannah."

"I don't need much, Mama, just little scraps is all. I can piece 'em together. I was wantin' to make some presents for the kids." I was not gonna share my plan just yet, so I looked out the kitchen window toward the small lean-to chicken coop next to the wood shed. Wes was scatterin' feed. Our Rhode Island Reds were scratchin' about, throwin' up dust. The Gravenstein apple trees behind the coop were bare and sad lookin'. The frosty winter garden was all bedded down in mulchin' straw. I washed the last dish and dried my hands.

"Behind my sewing basket there's some small scraps from what I'm working on now. It's not much, though," she said. "Take a look see."

"Thanks, Mama."

That's when there was a soft knock on the kitchen door. Mama was washin' up the half of Jesse's oatmeal that was on his face. "Can you get the door, Hannah?" She held her wet hands up for me to see and smiled.

"Sure, Mama." I pulled the door open and a scruffy man in patched up work clothes stood on the top step holdin' his crumpled hat in his hands.

"Good morning, young lady. Is your mama home?" Mama walked up behind me, wipin' her hands on her apron.

"Morning, Ma'am. I'm hoping you can spare a bite to eat. It's been two days, and I'd sure appreciate it." He looked down at his feet, and I hoped she would shoo him off. I shoulda' known better though. Men who rode the rails jumped off the train just before it came into the edge of town, so they stopped here from time to time, and Mama always tried to share what we had.

"Of course. Give me just a minute, and I'll see what I can find." She left me there holdin' the door. It was a kinda awkward silence until Wesley came scootin' past him with the egg basket not quite half filled with that mornin's eggs. Mama returned just then and the man spoke again.

"Looks like you could use some fire wood split. I'd be proud to do it if that's alright with you."

"I'm afraid we have no money to pay you," she told him as she handed him a half full bowl of oatmeal she had scraped from the pan.

"This here is pay enough, and I see the maul. Thank you, Ma'am." He turned toward the open door of the wood shed with his steaming bowl.

"Well, now, that'll be a weight off Papa's mind for a bit." Mama closed the back door. "Hannah, time to get goin'. Elizabeth! Wesley! Off to school now or you'll all be late."

Papa had been sittin' in his chair near the window, lookin' across the long stretch toward Thumb Butte. He hadn't said much since breakfast. "Hannah, 'fore you go, could you hand me that old newspaper on the wood pile? And Mama's scissors?"

"Sure, Papa." He kissed me on the forehead as I laid them in his lap.

"Hannah?" Mattie asked, "How many days to Christmas now?"

"Um?" I counted in my head. "Twenty-three, near as I can count. Hurry up, Lizzy!"

"Now get movin'! Don't be late," Papa said. Then we were out the door for our walk from the edge of town to the big red-brick schoolhouse on Gurley Street. It was cold out, so we moved fast as we could. The cold was soakin' through the cardboard in my shoes and my worn coat, and I knew Lizzy and Wes were feelin' the same chill.

I fingered the fabric scraps I had quickly stuffed into my pocket, a needle and thread tucked through them. I would start today at lunch recess.

Chapter Four

Papa was still in the living room near the window when we got home from school. The floor looked like a newspaper explosion. Cut up scraps of the *Prescott Evening Courier* were everywhere, and Papa had a row of empty tin cans lined up on the table beside him. One of them was cut up in odd pieces.

"What you doin', Papa?" Wesley asked. Mattie held up a chain of paper dolls Papa had cut for her out of newspaper, as if she had the answer to Wesley's question.

"Never you mind, son. It won't do to ask too many questions right before Christmas," Papa winked at Wes. "I already got in trouble once for usin' your Mama's good sewin' scissors on this paper. You don't want to put me in the dog house twice, do ya?"

"No, sir, Papa," Wes shook his head.

We took our shoes off and set them in front of the fire, then stood there a bit, wigglin' our toes, our hands stretched toward the welcome glow, warmin' up.

I looked over the fireplace to my favorite of Mama's embroidery sayin's. Two little sparrows sat on a leafy branch, their heads close together. "Keep your face always toward the sunshine and shadows will fall behind you," it said. It was Walt Whitman who said it, and Mama thought he was a right smart man.

"Mama's in the kitchen," Papa said after we'd warmed up a bit. "I expect she could use some help. Hannah, could you and Wes fetch some fire wood? Elizabeth, you can see what Mama needs."

Wes and I put our shoes back on. I kissed Mama as I passed through the kitchen. Wes and I hurried down the steps, so we could get back to the warmth of the fire.

"Children," Mama called after us, "tell Mr. Gomez I'll send him a plate soon as dinner's ready." Well, it looked like our company was stayin' on a bit. I suppose I wasn't surprised, knowin' Mama like I did.

"Yes, Mama," Wesley called back.

"What's Mama thinkin'? That's just one more mouth to feed." I mumbled without slowin' down a bit. Mama was too soft hearted to be sensible sometimes.

We loaded our arms with wood Mr. Gomez had spent the day splittin', and gave him Mama's message.

Inside again, I went upstairs and sneaked a few minutes to sew. I was happy with my first efforts, but I needed more fabric if my plan was gonna work.

'Bout an hour later Mama sent me back out with a bowl of watery beans and a piece of hot cornbread. It was dark, but the light from the kitchen windows was enough for me to see. Mr. Gomez had made a pallet in the corner of the shed on a pile of hay. A lantern hung from a rusty nail on the beam just above him. His hat was sittin' on the barrel of chicken feed and he was sittin' on an up-ended log round. He was reading, but he put his book down when I came through the shed door.

"Why thank you," he said, taking the food." You've been mighty kind. This sure smells good."

"Where you come from, Mr. Gomez?" I asked, knowin' for a fact Mama woulda said that was rude. I hadn't seen him around town before, so I was pretty sure he came in on the train.

"From Texas, on the Panhandle. Headed west to look for work, and I caught me a ride up the hill to Prescott. Thought I'd stay and rest my road weary feet a bit before moving on."

"What you readin'?" I nodded toward his worn book. Books always caught my curiosity.

" *All Quiet on the Western Front* by Erich Remarque, a fine book," he answered, holding it up so I could see it. It had a picture of a soldier on the front, big yellow letters announcing the title across the shirt of his olive green uniform. It held the mystery of faraway places.

"I like readin'," I said, "when I can get hold of a book. Guess I'm like Mama that way."

"It'll serve you well. The mind needs food sure as the body. What you got there?" He nodded toward the flowered fabric sticking out of my dress pocket.

"Just some scraps of fabric Mama had left over. Piecin' 'em together. Gonna make something for Christmas." I shrugged my shoulders. "It's hard to keep a secret in a house full of people."

"I expect so," he said, "but don't you think Christmas is a time for secrets?" Well, just easy as that I pulled the first, small, embroidered heart, done somethin' like what Mama called a crazy quilt, from my pocket and told him my whole idea for helpin' Santa.

Don't know what got into me, but there it was. He didn't seem to think it was so outlandish. Right there in the wood shed we came up with a plan for me to hide my sewin' behind the chicken feed barrel where nobody would discover it. My own Christmas secret.

"Seems like you need a bit more than that pocket full of fabric. How many have you made so far?" he asked.

"Just this one," I said, "Got two more started though. I'm working hard on my embroidery stitches." I held it up to the lantern light so he could see it better, suddenly feeling foolish.

"Looks like you've put a lot of love into it. Fine stitches for someone so young." He smiled at me gentle like, and it just felt like he understood. "Best get on back to supper now, before they worry where you went off to."

I waved kinda shy like and hurried back into the house for supper.

Chapter 5

I came down the stairs the next mornin' as Mama was fetchin' the milk bottles off the front porch. She set them on the kitchen counter and handed me a plate for Mr. Gomez. "Take this on out, Hannah, will you?"

"Yes, Ma'am," I answered, taking the plate. He was already at work splittin' wood, but he put the maul down when he saw me step out the back door.

"Here's breakfast," I said, balancing a plate with two hot biscuits and apple butter on the wood stack. "Sorry we don't have any coffee."

"Thank you. This right here is plenty good," he said. "Hannah? That's your name, isn't it? I have something here you might be able to use. Just yesterday I was helping your Papa repair the clothesline. That's not easy for a man on crutches. I mentioned what a soaking my bedroll got last time it rained with me out on the road. I've been keeping everything in an old feed sack, you see." He held up the printed fabric sack. "Well, your Papa gave me an old piece of oil cloth to wrap my bundle so I can keep things dry. I thought maybe you could use this here sack. Think it will work?" He handed me the sack and picked up a biscuit, takin' a bite. I ran my hand over the colorful cloth.

"You sure, Mr. Gomez? Must be a hundred good uses for a sack this big." I was admirin' the little flowers and vines printed on it.

"A traveling man needs to keep a light load," he answered. "It's hard to catch a moving train with your back weighed down. I'd be pleased to have you take it, seeing as how you're helping Santa."

It looked to be a 50-pound feed sack, enough fabric to make all the hearts I'd be able to finish by Christmas, if I was really fast. "Mr. Gomez, that's right nice of you. I expect I'll be sewing night and day."

"Best you get started then," he laughed. "And I'd best get back to this fire wood."

So, I kept a bit of sewing hidden in my pocket all the time after that mornin', stealing a minute here and there as I could. I sat on the schoolhouse steps, workin' tiny stitches, while the boys played Mumblety-PEG and the girls played jacks. I sewed through lunch recess or borrowed a few minutes off the end of an errand for Papa. Of course, Mama had in mind to help me find time to finish a heart for each member of the family since that's what she thought I was doin'. It pained me to have her think I was so terrible slow, but I didn't mind that she let me stay up sewin' half an hour after the younger ones were off to bed. I needed to keep a steady pace.

Chapter 6

Wasn't but a few days later us kids came home from school to find a Christmas tree sittin' in front of the living room window. It was a good tall pinon pine, almost touchin' the ceiling, without a single decoration. Papa was leanin' on his crutches with a crooked smile. He was holdin' a bulging burlap bag in one hand.

"Papa, where'd that come from?" asked Wes.

"Papa's ranch foreman came by to check in on him," Mama said. "Brought the tree and some canned peaches. Guess that means we'll be having peach pie for supper." A cheer went up for that news.

"But what's in the sack?" Wes persisted.

"Well, son, I climbed that ol' pine tree out front and brought us down some nice pine cones to decorate our tree," Papa said, handin' Wes the sack. We had a single tall Ponderosa Pine out front of our little house, and truth be told, there were cones just layin' in the yard to be gathered.

"Naw, Papa! You can't climb a tree with crutches," Mattie scolded him.

"Well, now, Mattie. Don't you go underestimatin' yer Papa," he said. "Nothin' wrong with my arms! I just threw me a rope up over a high branch and pulled myself up there, hand over hand, sure enough, gatherin' cones as I climbed. Look in the sack." He winked at me 'cause he knows I'm wise to him by now.

Mama gave us cotton string to tie the cones, and we went to work on makin' that tree beautiful.

Mama handed me a bowl of popcorn just as I finished puttin' up my second pinecone. "You can be in charge of stringin' the popcorn. Just push the needle straight through each one like this." She pushed the needle and a long white thread through the first one.

"Sure, Mama." I took the needle, knowin' that meant it would be awhile before I could get back to my sewin'. "Wes, get your hands out of the popcorn! It's for the tree," I scolded, swattin' at his hand.

"I'll get supper on," Mama said. "Stay out of the popcorn, Wesley James. You'll want to have room for that peach pie, and that's all the popcorn we have."

We had the pinecones and popcorn on the tree come supper time. It was kinda simple, but it looked nice to me. Mattie looked the tree over top to bottom and pulled my sleeve, "Hannah, how many days we got 'til Christmas now?"

"Mattie, Santa can hear every word you say," I told her. "You get on his nerves and he might decide not to come at all." That made her think a bit, and I figured I had at least a couple of days before she asked again.

"Hannah, Lizzy and Wes," Papa said, "bring me your shoes before we eat."

We pulled off our shoes, wonderin' what Papa was up to. One at a time he put them on a sheet of newspaper and drew an outline of the bottoms.

"What ya doin', Papa?" Lizzy asked.

"He's drawin' a picture of our shoes, Lizzy! Can't ya see?" Wes was always helpful like that.

"Is not," Lizzy said.

"Is so!" Wes insisted.

"Simmer down, now," Papa ordered. "I'm tracin' the sole of each shoe for a pattern so I can cut this here piece of old tire and fix you up good as new. I'll start with Hannah's when you get home from school tomorrow."

"You can do that?" Lizzy asked, plainly impressed.

"Well, Lizzy, Papa's gonna have a lot of time on my hands 'til I can get off these crutches and back to work. Wouldn't do to sit around gettin' in Mama's way for no good reason."

"Hannah," Mama called, "Can you please take this potato soup and pie out to Mr. Gomez?" The kitchen was warm and heavenly smellin'. I was sure hungry, but I needed to talk with Mr. Gomez.

"Be right back, Mama."

Chapter 7

Once every week Mama had me stop in at Mrs. Simms' place, about half a mile away. Mama said it was only right for us to look in on her now and then, since she had no family hereabouts. Mrs. Simms was a widow lady who lived on Pleasant Street, between our house and school. She had a pretty, white clapboard house with scalloped shingles on the gables, kinda like a fairytale house. Her husband had worked for the rail lines 'fore he passed on. I usually stopped in on the way home from school.

It was my visiting day, so I sent Elizabeth and Wesley on toward home as I bounded up the steps to Mrs. Simms' small porch. I tapped on the door even though she always said to just come on in.

"Mrs. Simms, it's Hannah," I called out. I tapped again and went on in.

"Hannah Meadows, you've grown an inch since I last saw you," Mrs. Simms said. "Come sit a spell, honey." Her hair was white, tied in a knot on top of her head, and she wore a pale blue, printed housedress and a hand knit cardigan sweater that looked like it belonged to someone bigger once.

"Thank you, Mrs. Simms." I settled into the loveseat across from her rocking chair. She had a small fire goin'. "Mama sent you a jar of her Gravenstein applesauce." I pulled the pint jar out of my lunch bucket and gave it to her.

"Well, bless her heart! Thank her for me," she said, putting the jar on the table beside her. "What have you been up to since our last visit?"

"Well, it's almost time for Christmas. I've been thinkin' on that some. Been makin' something."

"I don't expect most folks will be having much Christmas. Times is so hard," she said.

"I was wantin' to maybe help Santa a bit. I've been sewin'." I'd been visiting Mrs. Simms every week for over a year. I was sure I could trust her with my secret.

"What you makin'? Somethin' for the little ones?"

"Well, I guess you could say that." I pulled my latest heart from my dress pocket. "I need your help though." I put the half-finished heart in her hand. "I've been makin' these Christmas tree hearts to sell. Thought I could sell 'em out front of the Elks Opera House after folks come out from their picture show. You know Papa's out of work 'till his leg mends, and Mama's tryin' to sell some quilts she pieced to cover the bills."

"How can I help?" she asked. Mrs. Simms was a nice grandma-type lady that way.

"Would you mind if I sewed while we visit?"

"Not at all, honey," she assured me. "Why don't I cut while you sew?"

"But my fabric is at home," I reminded her.

"I have an old table cloth," she said. "It has a stain or two and a rip I can cut around, but it's nice fabric with some fine embroidery already on it. Let's get to work."

Mrs. Simms started cutting right there on her pine kitchen table, her knotted old fingers movin' with the skill of a lifetime of experience. By the time I had to leave for home she had 20 more ornaments cut out and she had come up with a plan for getting me to the Elks Opera House without Mama or Papa learning about my Christmas surprise.

I gave her a hug at the door. "Thank you, Mrs. Simms," I said, giving her a little wave as I hurried down the steps.

"Don't forget to drop off that feed sack on your way to school Monday. I'll get it ready for you, and I'll see what else I can find." She was still waving when I turned at the street corner off Pleasant and headed up Moeller Street. I ran most of the way home, my pocket bulging with finished hearts and others just waiting to be sewn.

With Mrs. Simms and Mr. Gomez helping, I was sure I could make Mama and Papa really proud of me. My plan was comin' together real nice.

Chapter 8

The next Friday I was back for a visit with Mrs. Simms. She had cut the feed sack into pieces the right size for her embroidery hoop and was workin' with her needle when I came in.

"Look here," she said, holdin up her hoop, "I been diggin' through my sewin' goods and come across a bundle of embroidery thread, and I found this red print from an old shirt of my Charles. Sit down and let me show you a new stitch or two, honey."

I pulled my work out and followed her example. "That's gonna be real nice, kinda fancy," I told her. "Oh, look here what Mama sent you," I said, pulling an apple out of my lunch bucket.

"It's sure enough a blessin' to have a root cellar," she said as she admired the apple, "and your dear Mama is good to share with me. What about Christmas dinner? Your Mama still got a pumpkin or two in the cellar?"

"Yes, Ma'am," I told her. "Mama says we'll have pie for Christmas. I can hardly wait." We sewed for just over an hour, and it was near time to get on home.

"Hard to believe we've come so far, honey. You get better with every heart you finish." She ran her hand across my stitches. "Now tell me, how's your Papa's leg comin' along?"

"He's not one to complain about it. I heard him tellin' Mama we should sell the pickup and just buy a bicycle soon as he's able to get back to work."

"Goodness! He wouldn't make it all the way to the ranch on a bicycle."

"Well, Mama said that made as much sense as catching one of the stray burros around town and using it. She said if he could figure how to get seven people on a bicycle, that would be just fine," I laughed, "but Papa didn't have an answer for that. So, Mama's been out sellin' eggs to neighbors who don't have chickens, and one of our neighbor ladies asked her to make a dress for her daughter's weddin'."

"Well, young lady, your Mama has the right idea. Eggs are ten cents a dozen, and that will sure enough add up. Now you best get on home before dark or your folks might just put us out of business." She gave me a hug and I was on my way, thinkin' the visit cheered us both.

Chapter 9

Papa had been spendin' a lot of time out in the shed with Mr. Gomez working on his own Christmas surprise. Mr. Gomez was real good at keepin' secrets, so all I knew was that Papa had been cuttin' up tin cans. I sure wasn't gonna press Mr. Gomez for information since I had somethin' invested in him keepin' my secret.

I knew Papa's only time to work on our shoes was at night when we weren't wearing 'em, and I could see scraps of rubber on the work bench. My shoes were finished already.

"It's chicken an' dumplin's tonight, Mr. Gomez. My favorite," I told him. Meat was a rare treat at our table and a chicken went a lot farther in dumplin's. It would be stretched out to feed us tomorrow, too. "You helpin' Papa mend our shoes?"

"No. I think your Papa has that well in hand though," he answered as I took a seat on one of the up-ended logs.

"Now that does smell delicious. Thank you, Hannah. Sit down a bit. How you coming along on your sewing?"

"I still need to do at least fifteen or twenty more hearts, I figure. Mrs. Simms cut 'em out for me though. Lizzy's Shirley Temple doll is $1.98. That's the small one, but it's the best I can manage. Wesley wants a Buck Rogers Space Ship 'cause he's crazy about that radio show, and that's near as much as Shirley Temple. Mattie's baby doll is $1.39, and a Teddy Bear for Jesse is 79 cents.

That's a whole lot of money, and most I can sell my hearts for is ten cents for the big ones. An' I got little ones that would be five cents each." I was sewin' as he ate his chicken an' dumplin's.

"Sounds like Mrs. Simms has been a big help," he said. He looked thoughtful as he ate.

"Yes, sir. She's cut everything out, and she taught me some new stitches. Now she's stitchin' some of the edges. Time's sure passin' though. Not sure I'm gonna make it."

"I think you will, but I expect your folks are waiting supper on you. Better tuck that away and get on in there."

"'Night, Mr. Gomez," I waved as I hurried out the door.

"Good night, Hannah. Don't you worry, now."

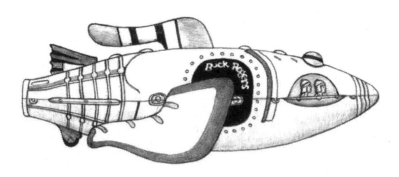

Chapter 10

A few nights later I was sittin' at the top of the stairs sewing quietly. It was a good place to get a bit of stairway light on my sewing without Mama or Papa seein' me. They had the floor radio on with Bing Crosby singin' "Silent Night, Holy Night". I could hear them talkin' all serious below, but the radio made them hard to understand. I leaned forward trying to hear better.

"Should be somethin' useful I could do, Sarah," Papa said, "that doesn't require two good legs. I just can't figure what it might be."

"I know, James, but jobs being what they are, it's just a bad time. Nothing we can do about it but cut every corner we can. You've given the children's shoes a bit longer, at least while they still fit. That's as good as money, don't you think?"

"I suppose," Papa said, "but it pains me to think of you sellin' those quilts. That's fine work, and it's taken you several years, workin' most every evening. You meant them for the children's Christmas. Here you are finally finished, and it just seems wrong is all." Papa sounded upset. Mama's quiltin' was a feast for the eyes, not just ordinary piece work.

"James," Mama reasoned, "I can make more quilts. We can't live without a house. The pastor's wife has offered to buy one, and I think I can sell two to the Larsons. They're the new couple on Park Avenue, just moved here from back in Arkansas. The house payment is $25.00, right?"

"That's right," Papa said.

"Well," Mama told him, "I can sell the quilts for $10.00 each. Then we worry about next month later. We'll think of something. You have to give your leg time to heal."

"And Christmas?" Papa asked. "What about Christmas? And what about the money we owe the doctor?"

"He said we could pay him with eggs and a couple of dressed chickens. I've taken eggs over twice," Mama said.

"Well, I'll get a chicken ready tomorrow then," Papa said. "That leaves Christmas, doesn't it?"

"We'll think on that. Let's get on up to bed now."

"Suppose we need to have a little faith," Papa said.

I made a quick retreat, quiet as a mouse. I could hear their footsteps startin' up the stairs as I eased the door shut on the room I shared with my brothers and sisters. Wes rolled over in the cot under the west window that he shared with little Jesse on the other end, but he didn't wake. There was a sliver of moonlight across the double bed I shared with Elizabeth on one end and Mattie and me on the other. Jesse sucked his thumb, as content as if there wasn't a trouble in the world.

Lookin' at the four of them sleepin', I knew what Mama and Papa were facin', and I knew my plan just had to work or it was gonna be a very sad Christmas. Seemed like I was never gonna have enough hearts finished to make a difference. I stitched awhile longer by that little bit of moonlight 'til I couldn't keep my eyes open any more.

Chapter 11

All the finished hearts were in a covered basket with four that still needed a bit of work. I placed the basket on the log end where Mr. Gomez usually sat and opened the lid. He took one out, cradling it in the palm of his weathered hand. As he turned it over, examining it closely, my confidence began to fade.

"I'm just no good at sewin', Mr. Gomez," I said, tears comin' to my eyes. "I've been doin' my best night and day, but I know they're nothin' like Mama's fancywork. "

"Hannah, they may not be what your Mama could do, but I expect she's had a good number of years to practice," he assured me. "These are very nice, but...".

"But nobody's gonna buy 'em, right? That's what you're thinkin'?" I sat down on the other log round, dead tired, covered my face with my hands and started to cry in earnest.

"Now, Hannah," he said. He placed a finger under my chin and lifted my head, lookin' me right in the eye. "I was going to say, they are very nice, but there is one more important thing left to do."

"But what else can I do? I'm out of material now, and I can't do Mama's fancy stitches." I wiped my nose with my pocket hanky.

"Nothing like that, child," he said patiently. He sat down on his log, puttin' the basket on his lap. "I'm thinking they need a blessing. That's all."

Now I was confused. "A blessing?"

"When you make something for somebody, part of what you give them is your skill and hard work." He picked up one of the hearts, holding it by the string that would suspend it from a tree branch. "Your stitches and the hours you have labored are all in here, and it shows. Those have value, but the real value in this heart is the love you've put into it, the love in your heart that keeps you working so hard night and day to help Santa. So, I was thinking we should ask a blessng over all this hard work."

"A blessing?" I asked again. "Do you mean like when we bless our food?"

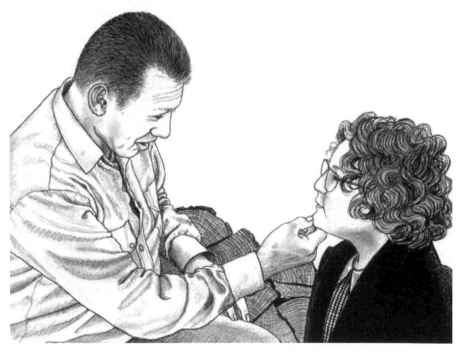

"Well, something like that. That kind of blessing is about being thankful," he said. "This kind of blessing is something you share with others. So, tell me, how many hearts are in this basket?"

"Forty-five big ones and thirty-two little ones," I said, wondering again if it was going to be enough to make a difference.

"So imagine seventy-seven people hanging one of these on their Christmas tree." His eyes twinkled as he continued. "They're each getting some of your hard work. That's a fact. They're each getting the love you put into creating a thing of beauty." He pressed the heart back into my cupped hands. "So if you sent each of these off to belong to someone new, what kind of blessing would you want to give those people?"

"You mean, what do folks need?" I asked. I was starting to get the idea. "I suppose lots of folks need enough to eat these days. Is that what you mean? Enough to eat, a warm bed, clothes to wear and shoes without holes in 'em. Well, and that they love each other like Mama and Papa love us. And then there's plenty of folks with no jobs, and there's folks like Mrs. Simms who are just lonely. And folks like Papa who have broken legs. And folks like you who need to get to a job somewhere far away. That's a whole lot of blessing for some plain little cotton hearts."

"Yes, that's true," he said, "but we can't underestimate the power of love. Christmas is all about the power of love, Hannah. Everybody needs love, and spreading love is the best way to be a blessing."

"How we gonna do that?" I asked, feelin' doubtful.

"Well, let's start by putting our hands right here on top of this fine work you've done," he said. I placed my hands on the basket heaped with those simple little scrap hearts.

I closed my eyes 'cause that's what Mr. Gomez did. "Bless Hannah's work," he whispered, "and fill it with whatever light, healing, comfort and blessing is needed by each person who receives it."

"And help folks that are hurtin'," I said, getting into the spirit of things. "And make sad people feel happy." I looked up at Mr. Gomez then, and he was smilin'.

"I expect getting one of these would make most folks happy. Look at that fine work. Your Mama taught you well." He laid the heart in the basket, and closed the lid once more. I couldn't tell that they were any different than before the blessing, but I had the feelin' Mr. Gomez knew what he was doin'.

"Good night, Mr. Gomez. Thank you for showin' me about blessing things," I said. "I expect that'll be a good thing to know growin' up." And I hurried back into the house.

Chapter 12

The day came that Mrs. Simms had asked Mama to let me spend the night and be some help around her house. Of course, Mama didn't know what the real plan was. Mrs. Simms and I had it all worked out. I had done my chores early, and I put on my coat. My nightgown was on the top of the basket, squishin' down the hearts. The ones that didn't fit were in my coat pockets, pushed down low.

"Seems like a mighty big basket for just one night," Mama said as she put her hand on the basket lid, givin' me a questioning look. "Why don't you take something smaller?"

"Well, Mama, I got my nightgown and clean underwear and my toothbrush. I still got Wes and Mattie's presents to finish, so I got a bit of sewing in there."

"Remember you're there to be a help to Mrs. Simms, not to do your own sewing," she reminded me. "Why don't you just leave your work at home? I expect you to be a blessing and not a bother, Hannah Grace."

"Yes, ma'am, I surely will. I'm set on bein' a real blessing, but could I maybe just take 'em to show her? She was askin' how they were comin' along." Mama had no idea how much of a blessing I was hopin' to be if I could just get out the door. I was purely relieved when she finally took her hand off the basket.

"I expect that won't hurt. Go on, then. Now, don't forget to brush your teeth, Hannah Grace," she said as she hugged me.

"Aw, Mama! I'm almost eleven years old. You have to go and say that?"

"Well, I expect not." Mama smiled, her hand gentle on my cheek.

"Give our best to Mrs. Simms," Papa said, "and give her those six eggs Mama wrapped up safe. Try to get there without breakin' 'em, young lady."

"Papa," I scolded, "You're bad as Mama. I expect I can get down the road in one piece and not crack any eggs on the way."

"Brush your teeth, Hannah, and don't break them eggs!" Wesley stuck out his tongue, and all the children laughed and waved goodbye.

I was out the door and on my way bright and early, thankful Mama or Papa hadn't looked into my basket. There was a lot left to be done before the movie matinee started that afternoon.

Chapter 13

Just as we'd been plannin', I walked the few blocks from Mrs. Simms' house on Pleasant Street to where I turned on Gurley Street toward the Elks Opera House, carrying my heavy basket. The opera house was a movie theater those days. The movie matinee that afternoon was "Confidential". I'd never been to a picture show, but the lady on the poster outside, Evalyn Knapp, was really pretty. There were gangsters from the mob and FBI men in the show. I didn't know much about that kind of thing.

I figured anyone like that must live in big cities. Folks who could afford 30 cents for a ticket would be coming out of the picture show in a few minutes.

I uncovered my treasures and found a place to stand just down the hill from the theater door. Some travelers would be stayin' across the street at the Hassayampa Inn. Others would be at the Hotel Saint Michael down the hill on the far side of the Courthouse square. Most everyone lived right near Prescott like me. Cars were parked along both sides of the street, and this looked like a place where lots of folks would have to walk by. I figured anyone who could afford a picture show could afford my little hearts, but I still asn't sure if they would want them.

"Excuse me, Ma'am," I called out to the first lady with a fine fur collar on her black wool coat. "Handmade Christmas decorations. Ten cents for a large one. Five cents for...."

"No, thank you," she said as she pushed past, bumping my basket. She crossed Gurley Street and disappeared into the Hassayampa Inn. I picked up hearts that had been knocked to the ground and tried again.

"Sir, buy a Christmas heart for your wife or your mama."

"How much?" he asked, pickin' one up.

"That size is ten cents. This smaller one is just five cents," I told him as he studied it closely, turning it over in his hand. "I made them myself."

"Delicate work," he said as he handed me a nickel. "Lovely fabric."

"Thank you, sir." I put the nickel in my coat pocket and turned to look for the next person. "Miss, would you buy a Christmas heart for someone in your family?"

"I'm in a bit of a hurry," she said without slowin' her pace at all, and she disappeared into the after-show crowd.

Three more people passed by without takin' the time to look, and I was beginnin' to get an awful feelin' in my stomach. This was not workin' out at all. If I couldn't even get their attention, then sellin' was hopeless. Tomorrow there would be a "Country Store" before the movie. It was a benefit for the Goodfellows Christmas Fund. That might bring a bigger crowd, but how would I get out of the house again?

"Mrs. Atherton! Would you like to buy a Christmas ornament for your daughter? I made them myself." Mrs. Atherton went to my church, so she stopped to look into the basket.

"Hannah, this is beautiful needle work. So lovely! Are you sure your Mama didn't make these?"

"No, Ma'am," I assured her. "I've been workin' on 'em for weeks. The big ones are ten cents."

"I'll take five," she said as she pulled out a fifty-cent piece. "Alice, look here. Can you believe this? Hannah Meadows made these."

"Yes, Ma'am, Mrs. Roberts. Two sizes to hang on your tree."

"Hannah, how did you do this? Where did you get these elegant fabrics? These tiny crystal beads? Surely your Mama doesn't realize you're selling them at this price. Hannah, you need to charge more." She opened her purse. "How many of the small ones do you have?"

Mrs. Atherton looked shamed as Mrs. Roberts waited for my answer. She pulled an extra nickel from her coin purse and dropped it my hand. "Mrs. Roberts is quite right. Come Sunday we must tell your parents how lovely your work is. Your Mama should be so proud of you."

"Thank you," I said. I was so flustered I couldn't remember how many small hearts I had made. "There are at least twenty-five small hearts, I think."

"I'll take them all for my own tree. Here's a dollar and fifty cents," Mrs. Roberts said. I hadn't even dreamed that one person would take so many, so I had nothin' to wrap twenty-five hearts. It didn't seem to matter. We counted them out, and she put them in the two large pockets of her expensive lookin' coat.

"Thank you and Merry Christmas," I said.

"Mr. Goldstein! Would you like to buy a heart for Mrs. Goldstein? Ten cents!" I knew Mr. Goldstein from his store on Cortez Street. He was a nice man who sometimes let people buy on credit when they didn't have money. Mama said our table would be mighty bare if not for him.

"Let me see, Hannah. What do you have here?" He turned one of the hearts in his hands, holdin' it up to the afternoon sunlight. "Yes, young lady. I think my dear wife would enjoy this. Is ten cents enough? It's quite delicate. No, let me give you a quarter, and I'll take one for my daughter, too."

I sold the others one or two or five at a time, and everybody studied them closely, exclaiming at how fancy they were. I was just plain mystified by all that excitement. I knew Mrs. Simms had helped me finish up that mornin', but she didn't stitch anything fancy either. All I could figure is it must a been somethin' about the blessing.

"Hannah Meadows? Hannah," someone called out as she pushed through the last of the picture show crowd. "There you are. I was afraid you would be gone," said my school teacher, Mrs. Simpson. "I just saw Mrs. Atherton. Please don't tell me you've sold out. This is what you've been working on during lunch recess, isn't it? Oh, my word!"

"Yes, Ma'am, Mrs. Simpson." I held out the nearly empty basket.

"I'll take eleven large ones. One for everyone in my family," she said. "Mrs. Roberts said they are twelve cents each. Hannah, I am so impressed. They're absolutely magical! Now I've finished all my Christmas shopping in one place."

Well, I knew for a fact they weren't magical, but they were surely blessed. By the time all the folks had returned to their cars or walked on home, I only had two small hearts left. All the big ones were gone. I wouldn't need to come back tomorrow. I just needed to do my shoppin' and hurry back to Mrs. Simms house to tell her the good news. I decided I would save the last two for Mrs. Simms and Mr. Gomez. I figured they both could use a blessing as much as anybody.

It had been a better day than I had ever dreamed possible, but now I had another problem. Mrs. Atherton was bound to see Mama at church service come Sunday, and my Christmas surprise would be ruined.

Chapter 14

I hurried down the block to Bashford & Burmister Company. Before going in I needed to count my money and check the window prices on each of the toys. There were two sizes of Shirley Temple dolls. I knew I would need to get the smaller one. I lifted the fistful of coins from my pocket. I couldn't even hold 'em all, but was it going to be enough?

I began stackin' my coins on the store's wide windowsill, arranging them by pennies, nickels, dimes and quarters. There was a fifty-cent piece. As I began to count, someone stepped into the store window display, and I watched as they removed the sign listing the toy prices. "Why is she takin' the sign?" I asked aloud.

"Could be they sold out," a lady said. "Maybe someone bought the last ones there in the window. I just hope there's a doll left for my daughter." She walked toward the door, and I glanced in her direction as she slipped inside.

Several doors down the hill, at the corner of Gurley and Montezuma Streets, I was sure I saw Mama. That was her blue coat. She was on her way into the Owl Drug and Candy Company. I ducked quickly into the shadow of the B&B doorway where the lady had just disappeared, keepin' a worried eye on my stacked money. I knew for sure Mama wasn't goin' to the soda fountain inside the Owl, so she must be gettin' some medicine for Papa's leg.

I couldn't take a chance that she would find me downtown when I was supposed to be helpin' Mrs. Simms. I quickly swept the stacks of coins back into my pocket. Then I hurried back up the street toward Mrs. Simms' house. "I'll just have to find a way back to the store on Monday," I reassured myself as I passed the opera house again in a breathless uphill rush. I went quickly past the arching stained glass windows of the Congregational Church, and headed toward Pleasant Street where Mrs. Simms lived.

I still needed to count my money, and now I was not even sure the toys would be there when I returned. "Please don't be sold out," I whispered.

Chapter 15

Come Sunday mornin' we were all lined up in our regular pew at the Methodist Church. I was lookin' around for Mrs. Atherton, hopin' maybe she felt sickly this mornin' and stayed at home. Well, that wasn't very Christian, I know, but it woulda solved my problem.

I bowed my head when the music started. No Mrs. Atherton yet. I was thankin' my lucky stars that my teacher went to the Congregational Church down the street a ways on the far side of the Courthouse square.

"Mornin', God. This here's Hannah Meadows. Me an' my family sit here in the fifth row by the stained-glass window most every Sunday. Remember me?

Please don't forget to bless the people who bought my hearts outside the picture show. I don't understand what all was goin' on there, but I'm pretty sure it was your doin'. Well anyway, thank you, and God, please give a special blessing to Mrs. Simms an' Mr. Gomez. Oh, and if you don't mind, I'd sure be obliged if you kept Mrs. Atherton away from Mama 'til we head for home. Amen."

"Hannah," Mattie leaned over and whispered, "Now don't go getting mad, but how many days we got left 'til Christmas?"

Right about then I was thinkin' God might 'preciate me bein' patient with Mattie. "Well, Mattie, this here's Sunday, and Christmas won't come 'til Wednesday. That's three more days. How 'bout I tell you right before it comes so you can stop worryin'?"

"Thanks, Hannah," she whispered. "Reckon Santa has presents for us?"

"Well, I don't know. You been good?" I asked her, all serious.

"Good as I can be, 'cept when I kicked Wes that time he stole my stick horse and hid it in the chicken coop," she said. "'Cause it was all covered with chicken poop." Lizzy, who was sittin' between us, laughed out loud right there in church.

"Well," I told her, "I expect Santa understands how tryin' a brother can be sometimes, 'specially our brother."

"You suppose he would understand about the time I ...?"

"Shhh!" Mama whispered, givin' us her I-mean-business stare. We hushed up.

The Christmas music was best it's ever been 'cept Mr. Mitchell, who sings terrible off key, but I was feelin' charitable so I sang loud enough to cover it up. Pretty soon Reverend Walters was givin' his message. I tried hard to concentrate, but my mind was on slippin' out without Mrs. Atherton talkin' to Mama or Papa. About the time the choir was singin' "Silent Night", I leaned across Lizzy and Mattie and whispered to Mama, "Mama, I've got a terrible bad stomach ache. Can we go home soon?"

"I'll tell Papa," she answered. "We'll hurry fast as we can."

We started for the door, but we had to do the usual greetin' and hand shakin' and pretty soon, Papa was sayin', "Good sermon, Reverend. Merry Christmas."

"Hope that leg mends quickly, James," the preacher said." Merry Christmas," and before you know it, we were out the door. I could see Mrs. Atherton across the crowd of church folks, but she was busy talkin' to the preacher's wife.

"Can we go now, Papa?" I asked again, and pretty soon we climbed into the pickup. Mama had to drive, what with Papa's leg and all. Papa and Jesse sat by Mama up front. Mrs. Simms was next to Jesse, 'cause we gave her a ride on Sundays when Papa was home. The rest of us bundled into old blankets in the back for the chilly ride home. I leaned against the cab to get out of the wind and pulled the blankets tight. Mrs. Atherton was hurryin' toward the pickup, callin' out to Mama just when we pulled onto the street. The cab was closed up tight against the cold, and Papa and Mama were both watchin' for traffic, so they didn't notice her. I was sure happy we made our escape.

"Thank you," I said, lettin' out the breath I'd been holdin'.

"For what? What'd I do?" Wesley asked.

"Never you mind, Wesley James."

Chapter 16

Monday mornin', December 23rd, I brought Mr. Gomez breakfast as usual. "Good mornin', Mr. Gomez. Hope you're stayin' warm enough out here," I told him. I could see my breath risin' in the air. "Corn meal mush today."

"Good morning to you, young lady," he said, taking the hot bowl to warm his hands.

"Mr. Gomez, Mama thinks I'm feelin' sickly 'cause of my stomach. I sort of had to tell a fib at church yesterday to keep my secret. It's a long story. Anyways, she told me I was to stay inside and rest today, and this is my only day to sneak to the B&B Company to go shopping before Christmas."

"I see. You suppose you could give me your list, and I could shop for you? Would that work?"

"That would work real good," I told him, pulling a hanky tied full of coins from my pocket. "Here's my money. I'd sure be pleased if you could do it."

"Well, it looks like you might have enough, don't you think?" He balanced it in his hand, sort of weighing how much it might be.

"I hope so, but I'm not sure." Then I told him all about what happened. The fancy fabric and beadwork on the hearts, and some folks even payin' more than I asked. I told him my shoppin' was cut short when I saw Mama at the Owl Drug and Candy Company and the lady pullin' the sign from the store window. I told him about Mrs. Atherton, and hidin' from her at church.

"Mr. Gomez, I don't know if the store sold Lizzy's doll or Wesley's rocket ship. Maybe all of the toys are gone. I got scared when I saw Mama. I wish I had just gone on in the store. I hope it's not too late. Could you just see what's left and get something they all might like. If there's money left, I reckon that'll ease Papa's worries."

"I expect it will. That's a good plan. It sounds like you had quite an adventure at the picture show, and at church," he said.

"Too much adventure for me." Then I remembered what was in my pocket. "Mr. Gomez, I got something for you." I handed him the small heart. "Nobody I'd want to give a blessing to more than you. Merry Christmas." I wrapped my arms around him and gave him a hug.

"Merry Christmas to you, Hannah." He hugged me back, then carefully tucked the heart into his shirt pocket. "It's been a joy getting to know you. I'll treasure this forever. It does seem to have a little extra sparkle." He held it up and it spun around on its string.

"You think so? I just see my plain ol' hearts."

"Well, the Good Book says that God is love, and we did ask for his blessing. All you see is your 'plain old hearts', but I'm thinking God has given other people eyes to see what's in your heart."

Well that mystified me, and I didn't know what to say. "Suppose I need to look again."

"Maybe so." He smiled.

"Oh, almost forgot. Mama says we'd be pleased to have you join us for Christmas dinner."

"Thank you. Your Mama's a fine cook, and your Papa has already asked me to dress a chicken. I expect it'll be quite a feast."

We talked a bit more about the shopping he would do. Those days nobody locked their doors, so we made a plan for him to put the gifts just inside the back door late on Christmas Eve, once all the lights were out. I wrote him a list on a scrap of paper. Then I went back inside to continue my long day of bein' sickly.

Chapter 17

By now I had gotten to be an expert at keepin' secrets and pretty good at bein' sickly. I was happy to be well again. Christmas Eve, Mama said I could go carolin' with the church young folks. Reverend Walters had put an announcement in the Prescott Evening Courier, asking for names of shut-ins who would enjoy a visit. Along the way, we sang *Silent Night* and *O Little Town of Bethlehem* for Mrs. Simms, and she waved to us from her living room window.

I got home about the time Mama and Papa were ready to call it a night. I went to bed, too, actin' all sung-out and sleepy, and before long I could hear snorin' from their room. I tiptoed to the end of the hall and back down the stairs. I stepped over the third step from the bottom that had a squeaky board, makin' my way across the living room. Once I had crossed the kitchen to the back door, I could see the packages. God bless Mr. Gomez. He had wrapped 'em all in plain brown paper, tied with red ribbon. I looked at the little tags on top, all neatly hand written. "To Elizabeth or Wesley or Mattie or Jesse, from Santa", they each said.

The room was dark with just a soft glow from the banked fire Papa left, so I was careful not to bump anything as I tucked gifts under the tree and went on back to my bed. I was too excited to fall asleep 'til near mornin'.

I couldn't see it, but I thought of Mama's stitched picture on our bedroom wall and smiled. It said, "There was never a child so lovely but his mother was glad to get him to sleep." I wondered if Ralph Waldo Emerson coulda known this sleepless night was comin'.

"Hannah, wake up! It's Christmas." Elizabeth shook me until my eyes opened. "Hurry, get up."

Wesley was already out the door and half way down the stairs. Mattie and Jesse were sittin' up, wide eyed. "Did Santa come?" Mattie asked.

"Well, let's go find out," I told them, and we all raced after Wes in our night clothes.

"What's all this racket?" Papa asked, wrappin' his robe around him.

"Good heavens!" Mama said as she reached the bottom step and could see the Christmas tree. "What on earth? James, what is this?"

"Santa!" Elizabeth and Wesley shouted together. "Santa came!"

"I don't rightly know, Sarah," Papa looked at Mama, just as confounded as she was.

On top of the tree was a punched tin angel with delicate designs on its skirt and wings. The mantel held two punched tin lanterns, with candles glowin'. I figured that was what Papa and Mr. Gomez had been workin' on in the wood shed. It was real fine work.

Our stockings hung from nails on the mantel. They weren't stockings like folks hang nowadays, but just our regular socks. Best we could do was look for one with no hole in it. Each of our stockings had an orange, one stick of candy from Santa and a punched tin Christmas decoration. They were made out of can lids and had fancy designs like stars and flowers in the middle, their edges all crimped and curled in fanciful scrolls. They had been tied with string saved from feed sacks.

"Santa gave me this star!" Wesley said. "Can I hang it on the tree?" We all hung our stars or flowers on the tree, and it looked mighty festive. I had never seen such a beautiful Christmas tree.

"The angel," Mama said, "It's beautiful, James. Don't think I've seen a prettier one anywhere." Then she dropped her eyes again to the packages under the tree. Looked to me like she was gonna cry. "Somebody please explain this to me."

"'Splain to me, how Santa got past the hot coals in the fireplace," Mattie insisted. "That's what I wanna know."

"Now Mattie, nobody told you 'bout Santa's special fire-proof boots?" Papa asked.

"That true, Mama?" Mattie asked.

"Would your Papa tell a lie?" Mama asked, like that was just plain outlandish. "I expect Papa knows what he's talkin' about, don't you?"

Papa started pickin' up packages and readin' names, "To Elizabeth from Santa," and on down the list of kids 'til each of them had a package. Mama was wipin' her eyes. "To James, Love Sarah." He read, and looked over at Mama.

Then Papa looked beneath the tree again. I knew he was lookin' for a package for me, and I was gonna be hard put to explain that. As for me, though, I was happy with the orange, stick of candy and tin flower. I knew how hard Mama and Papa were tryin' just to keep us fed.

"Santa brought me a baby doll, Mama," Mattie said. "Look, Papa." She held the small doll up for inspection.

"I got me a Buck Rogers Space Ship, just like at the store!" Wes shouted, flyin' it through the air above his head, doin' his best to make space ship noises.

"What did Jesse get from Santa?" Papa asked.

"My Teddy," he said as he crawled carefully up onto Papa's good leg, holdin' the furry brown bear.

"Santa gave me Shirley Temple!" Lizzy squealed. "Mama, Papa, look at her dress. Her eyes move and she has curls and a real autographed Shirley Temple photograph."

"She's lovely," Mama said.

"Papa, what did you get?" Wesley asked.

Papa held up a fine pair of warm leather work gloves. "Looks like I won't be wearin' socks on my hands when I'm out ridin' anymore. These are some fine warm gloves." He smiled at Mama that special way he does. Now I knew the secret of the small package from the B&B Company.

"Well, children," Mama finally found her voice and stood up, "It's time for some breakfast. Hannah, I think it would be nice to ask Mr. Gomez to join us this mornin'."

"Yes, Mama," I agreed. I was plenty happy to slip out the back door. I ran down the steps toward the wood shed. "Mr. Gomez, Merry Christmas!" I knocked, then pulled the shed door wide. "Mama says...," but the shed was empty. He wasn't there. His bedroll and all his other things were gone. On the feed barrel was a small package with a red ribbon and a folded piece of paper. When I unfolded the note a few coins tumbled out onto the top of the barrel.

"Hannah, this package is for you. Merry Christmas, my dear young friend. Now I hope you never forget that love is always the best, most beautiful gift you can give. Please thank your folks for taking in this stranger and being so kind. By the way, I was just in time for the big 'Last Minute Christmas Sale' at the B & B Company, so you got Lizzy's Shirley Temple doll, Wesley's space ship and just what the little ones wanted. This extra seventy cents was left. I expect your folks will find a good use for it."

Papa's tools were all sharpened and even the two log rounds we had used as seats had been split. Other than that, the shed was as tidy as if he had never been there at all. It sure felt empty.

I picked up the package and the coins, and I went back to the house.

Chapter 18

After cleanin' up from a special Christmas breakfast of fresh baked cinnamon rolls and milk, Mama turned to me. "Hannah, Papa can keep an eye on the little ones. You come with me to pick up Mrs. Simms for Christmas dinner. I have a feeling you might know somethin' I don't. I think it's time we had a little talk."

"Yes, ma'am," I said, but I just stared at the floor. With Mr. Gomez gone, it didn't seem real. To tell the truth, I was feelin' sorrowful he was gone. Mama grabbed the pickup keys off the hook by the kitchen door, and I followed her outside.

"We'll be back shortly, James," Mama called over her shoulder. "I expect everyone will be busy playin' for that long."

Once we settled into our places and Mama fired up the old pickup, there was no more stallin' for time. Mama drove just a bit, then pulled to the side of the road down a ways from our house and turned off the engine.

"Hannah, please tell me where the toys came from, and don't say, 'Santa'. Tell me what happened to the hearts you have spent over a month working on, and what was the package you brought in from the shed? What on earth is going on?"

"I'm sorry, Mama. I was just tryin' to help Santa is all. I had the scraps you gave me, and Mr. Gomez gave me a feed sack to use, and Mrs. Simms gave me an old torn table cloth and a shirt that had been her husband's, and I guess I just kept sewing...." I told her the whole story, about the toys the children wanted Santa to bring, and workin' on all the pieced-together hearts, and Mr. Gomez teachin' me about bein' a blessing, and spendin' the night with Mrs. Simms and the picture show. Time I was done, she had the whole story right up to the empty shed and Mr. Gomez bein' gone.

"What was in the package?" Mama asked softly.

"It was a book I was dreamin' of, **Caddy Woodlawn**. Don't know how he knew. A brand-new book all my own, Mama. Just for me. It smells like learnin'."

"I don't expect there's a thing in the world that would make my girl more pleased," Mama said. "But tell me about the hearts again. What do you mean, 'They changed after the blessing?'."

"Mrs. Simms can show you. I gave her and Mr. Gomez the two I didn't sell."

So we took off again for Mrs. Simms' house, and after Mama saw the fancy heart sparklin' like it did, she never doubted my story once. Turned out one side of every heart was just like I made it. Mama and Mrs. Simms said it was work to be proud of, just like that. The other side, when you turned it over, was the fanciest thing Mama said she'd ever seen. This time I thought maybe I could see it, too, cause I surely understood I loved my family.

"Like the needlework of angels," Mama said. "Could it be Mr. Gomez was workin' for Santa?"

"It's sure enough a mystery," Mrs. Simms said as we got back into the pickup.

"Hannah," Mama said as we drove on down the street, "That was a fine, generous thing you did. I am so proud of you." That made me feel good all the way to my toes, even more than the sparkles.

So, we headed back home for roast chicken, mashed potatoes, gravy, pickled beets from last summer's garden, Mrs. Simms' gingerbread and Mama's pumpkin pie. It was a feast to remember. To this day, I believe it was the best Christmas we ever had.

Wasn't much after that Mama put up a new sayin' right over the kitchen door. It was embroidered like as if it was tied in red ribbon, with a small gold heart just hangin' there above the words. "Be not forgetful to entertain strangers: for thereby some have entertained angels unawares. Hebrews 13:2"

We never heard from Mr. Gomez again after that Christmas of 1935, but I like to think he carried my heart with him when he headed off that mornin', and I hope he knew what a blessin' he had been to a little girl named Hannah Grace Meadows, and to one Prescott, Arizona family.

Be not forgetful to entertain strangers:
for thereby some have entertained
angels unawares.
Hebrews 13:2

Locations Mentioned in *Hannah's Heart*

In 1935, Prescott, Arizona had a population of about 5,000. It was truly a small ranching town. Gurley Street divided the city north and south, while Cortez Street divided the city east and west. There were about 25 grocery stores, many of them small neighborhood markets.

Buildings mentioned in the story are all within walking distance of the Courthouse Plaza.

First Congregational Church

Historical fiction draws from real places and real events in history to create a story with imagined characters and imagined events. In this story, Hannah's teacher went to First Congregational Church. This very real, beautiful brick building with its arching, stained glass windows, is located at 220 East Gurley Street, right next to Washington School.

The First Congregational Society of Prescott, Arizona was organized on September 26, 1880, with the Rev. Dr. Warren, Missionary Superintendent for Southern California, and a group of thirteen interested Prescott residents. They met in the home of T. W. and Pamela Otis.

The new congregation met in the Methodist Church building on Marina Street until their building was complete. The First Congregational Church, which is still active in the life of the City of Prescott, is the oldest Congregational Church in the state of Arizona.

There was an early emphasis within the Congregational Church on free public education without the requirement of religious instruction, and there were several educators within the early Prescott membership. It makes sense that First Congregational would have been a good church home for Hannah's fictional teacher.

The church parsonage still sits next to this historic building from Prescott's early days.

Westside Methodist Church

Between 1864 and 1866, Rev. Hiram Reed lead the first Protestant Sunday School and worship services near Granite Creek with the ringing of an iron triangle that was hung just outside the building known as Fort Misery in the settlement of Prescott.

By December 1870 Rev. Alexander Gilmore, a Northern Methodist minister, had arrived to serve as chaplain at Fort Whipple. Rev. Alexander Groves arrived very soon after, and these two pastors held regular weekly services. By 1872 the Methodist Church South had begun construction of the first Protestant church in the state of Arizona on Marina Street. They found they did not have sufficient funds to complete the project, so they deeded it to the Methodist Church North. These North and South titles were indications of the separation within the Methodist Church on the issue of slavery. In spite of this difference, the two congregations worked together in many ways.

In the spring of 1876, Henry Fluery donated the property on the corner of Gurley and Summit Streets to the Methodist Episcopal Church South, and the first service was held on Christmas Eve of that same year. The two congregations continued to work together.

The Methodist Church North, located on Marina Street, was used by Presbyterian, Baptist, Congregational, Episcopal and Roman Catholic congregations as they each established a presence in Prescott. They would each soon build their own churches.

That building burned down because of an overturned oil lamp in August 1891. The congregation soon raised another building close by on Marina Street.

In 1935, the church on Marina Street was really struggling, and was forced to close its doors. The two Methodist (North and South) congregations united at the Gurley Street address.

The Marina Street building was sold to the Nazarene Church in 1939, the last year of the Great Depression. That was also the year Northern Methodists and Southern Methodists nationwide would unite as one denomination. Today Prescott United Methodist Church continues to worship at 505 West Gurley Street.

Other 1935 Congregations

The *City Directory of Prescott, 1935-36* had listings for 22 church congregations. Two of those congregations were in Miller Valley. Of the remaining twenty congregations, six were on Marina Street and four were on Gurley Street. Congregations worshiping in the Prescott area included Church of Christ Christian, Church of God (Non-Sectarian), Church of Jesus Christ of Latter Day Saints, Church of The Nazarene, First Baptist Church, First Christian Church, First Church of Christ Scientist, First Congregational Church, First Methodist Episcopal Church, First Pentecostal Church, Lutheran Church, Mercy Hospital Chapel, Peoples AME Zion Church, Presbyterian Indian Mission, Sacred Heart Church (Catholic), Sacred Heart of Mary (Catholic, Mexican), Saint Lukes Episcopal Church, Salvation Army Citadel, Trinity Full Gospel Church and West Side Methodist Church.

Prescott Train Depot

The first railroad track to Prescott was completed on December 31 of 1886, but the Mission Revival style Santa Fe depot was not completed until September of 1907. It was built by Frank M. Murphy at the very north end of Cortez Street where the Santa Fe, Prescott and Phoenix Railway came to town. It was the arrival place for freight and passengers to Prescott for exactly 100 years. The last train arrived on Dec.31, 1986.

Today the depot, beautifully restored in 1990, is the focal point of the Depot Market Place, providing professional offices to local businesses.

Yavapai County Courthouse

The current Yavapai County Courthouse stands at 120 South Cortez in the beautiful Courthouse Plaza. Construction was started in October of 1916 and completed in September of 1918. The building was designed by architect William N. Bowman of Denver, and built by Rogers & Ashton, also from Denver. Italian stonemasons were brought in to create the Neo-classical Revival Style building from locally quarried granite.

This plaza is the central focus of Prescott's Christmas celebrations, when the building and entire area of surrounding trees are spectacularly lighted.

Elks Theatre

The classically designed Elks Opera House was completed in 1905. It is located a short walk from the Courthouse Plaza at 117 East Gurley Street. Over the decades it has offered live theatrical performances, minstrel shows, vaudeville acts, silent pictures, musical performances and movies. After several remodels over the years, the building has been beautifully restored to its earlier glory and hosts many community events. It is now owned by the nonprofit, the Elks Theatre and Performing Arts Center.

Bashford & Burmister Company

The Bashford & Burmister Company advertised itself as "Dealers in Everything", and they were in fact an early version of today's department stores. The B & B sold mining equipment, hardware, furniture, firearms, groceries, flowers, toys and more. It was located on Gurley Street across from the courthouse. The Bashford & Burmister partnership was established in 1874 as a large mercantile store. That original structure burned down in the fire of 1900. The new brick building was erected after the fire, and enlarged and remodeled in 1929, in the current Art Deco style.

The Bashford & Burmister buildings have housed a variety of businesses over the years, from tiny shops to larger stores and restaurants, creating one of the interesting places to explore and shop in Prescott's historic downtown.

Owl Drug and Candy Company

From roughly 1915 until the mid-1940s, the Owl Drug and Candy Company was on the northwest corner of Gurley and Montezuma Streets, just off the Courthouse Plaza. The drug store, candy store, bakery sales and soda fountain were at ground level. The candy and ice cream factory was in the basement. This business was opened as a partnership between Ed Shumate and pharmacists, Albert William Bork Sr. and Leon C. Corbin, and eventually taken over by Mr. Shumate and his son. The Owl was a popular meeting place for Prescott residents. The building has held a variety of businesses over the years.

Hassayampa Hotel

The elegant Hassayampa Hotel is a Spanish Colonial Revival style red brick building with Italianate influences. It was designed by Southwest architect, Henry Trost, and completed in 1927. It has many charming details, but the hand-painted ceilings and wall murals are impressive.

Located on the north west corner of Gurley and Marina Streets, it was renovated in 1985. The Hassayampa has hosted such famous guests as George W. Bush, Clark Gable, Tom Mix, General John Pershing and Will Rogers.

Hotel Saint Michael

The gracefully arched windows and red brick exterior of Hotel Saint Michael dominate the south west corner of Gurley and Montezuma Streets, with stern gargoyles overlooking tourists below. This historic hotel was built in 1901 with a view of the Courthouse Plaza.

Many famous guests have enjoyed a stay at Hotel Saint Michael, including the Earp brothers, Doc Holiday and Billy the Kid of frontier fame, and Theodore Roosevelt and Barry Goldwater.

Washington Traditional School

Washington School was built in 1903 to replace Arizona Territory's first public school, Prescott Free Academy.

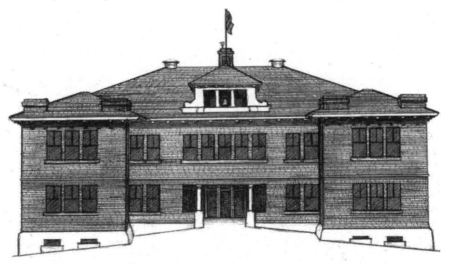

It was constructed directly behind the existing school and opened to students on Sept.1, 1903. The older school was then torn down. The bell from Prescott Free Academy was transferred to the new, three story facility.

Washington Traditional School is the oldest school in continuous use within Yavapai County and one of the oldest in Arizona. It now houses Prescott Unified School District's Discovery Garden Preschool, the Family Resource Center

Acknowledgements

The following people have supported this book in many ways, helping me to create something far better than I could have without their contributions. Elisabeth Ruffner was a very helpful and generous source of information concerning Prescott history as well as introducing me to others who could help. I'm indebted to the staff at the Sharlott Hall Museum Library and Archives and Prescott Public Library staff as well. Ron and Nancy Fein, Gail Steiger and Virginia Seaver were gracious and very generous with information about ranch life and ranch history in Arizona. Rev. Stan Brown was my generous source of information about Methodist Church history in Prescott. Rev. Dan Hurlbert provided information about Prescott United Methodist Church and gave me the gift of several *Prescott Evening Courier* newspapers from the 1930s. Rev. Jay Wilcher and church historian, Jay Eby were very accommodating with information concerning First Congregational Church.

Parker Anderson provided important information about the Elks Opera House. Tom Brodersen and Rabbi Jessica Rosenthal were very helpful with information about Jewish history in Prescott. Deb Walker and Sylvia Neeley were generous sources of information concerning Washington School during the Great Depression. Bill Neeley shared important information about childhood during the Depression.

Regina Younger was a real source of encouragement and ideas, introducing me to or going with me to meet people who are the ones who lived Prescott history so that I had as many family accounts as possible. Those who read drafts of the story and helped me to move it forward to something I could be proud of were Mary Lea Adkins, Betty Arnold, Cynthia Brown, Nancy Ethridge, Rev. Gary Gard, Rev. Darrel Gilbertson, Pat Graham, Jessi Hans, Gail Haugland, Susan Lowe, Karen Murphy, Barbara Polk, Kelley Poynter, Elisabeth Ruffner, Shirley Warrick, and Savannah Webster.

Special thanks to Charlie Medina, Rob and Gretchen Whittaker and their children (Reagan, Adam, Cate and Kyllian), and Keagan, Sailee and Jonas Hans, who made this book come to life. Karen Murphy was unbelievably generous with her time and knowledge about community resources and in moving forward my hope of turning *Hannah's Heart* into a stage play. Melanie Ewbank Snyder willingly applied her gifts to that dream, for which I will be forever grateful. Barbara Polk has been the loving, positive friend and blessing everyone needs when they reach for something above and beyond their ability. Gail Haugland was on board from beginning to end with everything that was needed, from thoughtful feedback to embroidery and Depression-era crafts. She has been a true wonder. Donna Gaddy and Leigh Downing were support and encouragement in many ways. Jessi Hans has been a joy and a blessing, always thoughtful.

Denise Domning shared her expertise as an author of many books, helping me along the way on a new venture.

I thank my inspirational friend , Paul Mitchell, for supporting this idea. He has been a visionary friend in many ways. Thanks also to the ladies of Hillside Church of God, Prescott, Chino Valley and Prescott Valley United Methodist Women and American Lutheran Women, hands that serve by sewing.

Then there is Doug Iverson, my husband, who understands the obsession with researching a topic that takes over when a book is being created, edits patiently, is a good cook and much more than that. He's my safe place.

Thanks to my grandparents, Virgil and Lula Mae Wall, who taught me about the kind of love that shines brightly, and to the real Mr. Juan Gomez, from Kerman, California, who left a box of Christmas toys on our porch. You were a blessing.

This is the way a book is born, with a circle of blessing, kindness, skill, expertise, patience and energy that allows an author's dreams to thrive and grow into something with pages that you can hold in your hands, far beyond what one person could ever hope to create alone.

Written Resources

Willow Creek Road, The Story of Three Brothers on an Arizona Ranch, Richard Clark, One World Press, 2003

Prescott: A Pictorial History, Melissa Ruffner, Primrose Press, 1981

The Prescott Evening Courier, www.d.courier.com/pre-website-archives/

City Directory of Prescott, 1935-36

Book Group Discussion Questions:

- Read the first chapter of the book aloud in your discussion group. Do you know anyone who lived through the Great Depression? Were their experiences similar to those in *Hannah's Heart*?

- Why was the Great Depression difficult for families like Hannah's?

- How was Hannah's world different from a ten-year-old child's life today? How was it the same?

- Does any character in the book remind you of someone you know?

- If you could be a character in the book, who would you want to be?

- If you could meet someone in the book and talk to them, what would you like to say?

- How is the town of Prescott, Arizona the same as or different from the place where you live?

- What part of the book stands out most clearly in your thoughts? Why?

- What one word would you use to describe Hannah? Mr. Gomez? Mama? Papa? Mrs. Simms? Hannah's younger brothers and sisters?

- Do you think Hannah grows or changes in the story? How?

- What ways were people in the story resourceful when they didn't have money?

- What examples do you remember within the story of people helping each other through the difficulties of this Great Depression Christmas?
- How can people be of help today when they know someone who is out of work or struggling to put food on the table for their family?
- Was the ending what you expected? If you wrote the ending, how would it be different?
- Would you recommend this book to someone else? Why or why not?

Ten Ways You Can Help Low-Income Families

1. Donate food, clothing or money to a service for low-income families where you live. Many such services have thrift stores, so it is helpful to donate serviceable used clothing and household items as well.

2. Your class, scout troop, or church group can do a toy drive for Christmas or a coat drive for winter. Donate these items to a service organization in your area. If your area does not have such an event already, maybe you will want to help organize one.

3. Be kind to kids who are left out or made fun of. Always refuse to be part of bullying.

4. If you live where you can plant a garden, encourage your family to plant a little extra. Donate fresh fruits and vegetables to your local shelter or food bank.

5. The next time you have a birthday party, ask your friends to bring a gift for a child in need. Donate those gifts to a family shelter near you.

6. Hold a book drive. Ask for new or gently used children's books. Share the books with a children's literacy group, a family shelter or food bank. You may even set up a Little Free Library at your church or other organization. For inspiration go to https://littlefreelibrary.org/. Books are a luxury for families struggling to buy groceries.

7. Ask your school, club, or church to sponsor a production of the play, ***Hannah's Heart***. See ***It's a Play!*** on the following

page for information. Donate a portion of the ticket price to a nonprofit serving low-income families in your area.

8. Ask your librarian for other books about children living in poverty and service projects kids can do.

9. When you are shopping for back-to-school supplies, ask your parents to fill an extra backpack for someone who can't afford one. You can help earn the money for supplies through the summer by doing odd jobs like watering plants or feeding pets for a neighbor on vacation. Deliver the filled pack to your school office. Tell them it is for anybody who needs it. The fun part is to keep it a secret so nobody knows it was from you. A gift given without needing credit is the very best kind.

10. **Donate to Coalition for Compassion and Justice on line at yavapaiccj.org, or at Coalition for Compassion and Justice, PO Box 1882, Prescott, Arizona 86302. Thanks for caring!**

It's a Play!

Hannah's Heart is also available as a play script. For information or to purchase, please contact playwright, Melanie Ewbank, at **writer@melanieewbank.com** .

Melanie Ewbank is an award-winning playwright and actress. Her plays have been produced in festivals in Los Angeles, CA, Arizona, and Idaho, and several of her longer one-acts toured LA area prisons, juvenile detention centers, and assisted living facilities. A staged reading of her full-length play, *I Found Baby Jesus in the Cat Box,* was produced by Pasadena Playhouse, and her one-act play, *Platitudes of Perfect-ness,* took first place in Knoxville Writer's Guild's 2012 writing contest. As an actress, Melanie has won an LA Weekly Award, a Charlie Award, and has been twice nominated for the prestigious Garland Award.

About the Author and Illustrator

Diane Iverson was born in Fresno, California and raised just outside the small San Joaquin Valley farming town of Kerman. She grew up on a small cotton, alfalfa and dairy farm.

Diane is the author and/or illustrator of over 20 books. Her illustrations are in the permanent collections of the Arne Nixon Center for the Study of Children's Literature (Fresno, California) and the Mazza Museum of International Art from Children's Books (Findlay, Ohio). She works primarily in colored pencil on Bristol board, or, as in this book, she also enjoys rendering in pencil.

Diane is a founding member of the Coalition for Compassion and Justice, a nonprofit that addresses the needs of low-income residents in Yavapai County, Arizona. She is the recipient of the 2016 Albert Lovejoy Social Justice Award.

Diane and her husband, Doug Iverson, have made their home in Prescott, Arizona since 1996. They have two daughters and seven grandchildren.

Diane is a popular speaker at schools and other organizations. Contact the author at **ldianeiverson@gmail.com**.

Other Books by Diane Iverson

- *I Celebrate the World*
- *Buttons the Foster Bunny* (written by Teddi Grover)
- *I Celebrate Nature*
- *Discover the Seasons*
- *My Favorite Tree*
- *Forest Alphabet Encyclopedia* (written by Sylvester Allred)
- *Earth Notes* (illustrations only)
- *Nature's Restoration* (written by Peter Friederici)
- *We Like to Move* (written by Elyse April)
- *We Like to Help Cook (*written by Marcus Allsop)
- *Desert Alphabet Encyclopedia* (written by Sylvester Allred)
- *Rascal: Tassel-eared Squirrel* (written by Sylvester Allred)
- *Freshwater Alphabet Encyclopedia* (written by Sylvester Allred)
- *The Mystery of Blackbird Pond*
- *Ready to Wean* (written by Elyse April)
- *Cimarron the Bighorn Sheep* (written by Sylvester Allred)
- *When I Dream*
- *Sheena's Kiss* (written by Wendy Ratner)
- *Josie, a Story of Faith and Survival* (with Susan Lowe)
- *Jabber, The Steller's Jay* (written by Sylvester Allred)

Support Compassionate Solutions
for Children Living in Poverty

When I Dream, a moving, full color, 32 page picture book about a homeless little girl with big dreams, is available through the **Coalition for Compassion and Justice, PO Box 1882, Prescott, Arizona 86302** for $12.00 including postage and handling. Please send your check with return address. This book has been donated by the author/illustrator and all funds go to provide services for families in need within Yavapai County, Arizona.

Made in the USA
Las Vegas, NV
31 October 2020